*Rimbaud
the Son*

Rimbaud
the Son

PIERRE MICHON

TRANSLATED BY JODY GLADDING AND

ELIZABETH DESHAYS

YALE UNIVERSITY PRESS ■ NEW HAVEN & LONDON

A MARGELLOS
WORLD REPUBLIC OF LETTERS BOOK

The Margellos World Republic of Letters is dedicated to making literary works from around the globe available in English through translation. It brings to the English-speaking world the work of leading poets, novelists, essayists, philosophers, and playwrights from Europe, Latin America, Africa, Asia, and the Middle East to stimulate international discourse and creative exchange.

Cet ouvrage a bénéficié du soutien des Programmes d'aide à la publication de l'Institut français. (This work, published as part of a program of aid for publication, received support from the Institut Français.)

Published with assistance from the Mary Cady Tew Memorial Fund.

Yale University Press books may be purchased in quantity for educational, business, or promotional use. For information, please e-mail sales.press@yale.edu (U.S. office) or sales@yaleup.co.uk (U.K. office).

Set in Electra and Nobel types by Keystone Typesetting, Inc.
Printed in the United States of America.

Library of Congress Cataloging-in-Publication Data
Michon, Pierre, 1945–
[Rimbaud le fils. English]
Rimbaud the son / Pierre Michon ; Translated by Jody Gladding and Elizabeth Deshays.
  pages cm
Originally published in French as Rimbaud le fils, Éditions Gallimard, Paris, 1991.
ISBN 978-0-300-17265-2 (alk. paper)
1. Poets, French—19th century—Biography. 2. Rimbaud, Arthur, 1854–1891—Family.
I. Title.
PQ2673.I298Z711513 2013
841'.8—dc23
2013012746

A catalogue record for this book is available from the British Library.

10 9 8 7 6 5 4 3 2

There is a whole epoch between us and, today, an entire
country of snow.
—Mallarmé

CONTENTS

TRANSLATORS' INTRODUCTION

Take it into your head to write a preface to Rimbaud, writes Pierre Michon, and your wings fall off; you start quoting the saints of the almanac. Duly warned, we proceed with caution and will be brief. *Rimbaud le fils* (Rimbaud the Son) was published in France in 1991, seven years after Michon's first book, *Vies minuscules* (Small Lives). *Vies minuscules* won Michon immediate acclaim and was quickly followed by other successes; *Rimbaud le fils* was his fifth published work. Although still relatively unknown to readers in the United States, Michon is widely recognized in Europe as one of France's foremost contemporary writers. He won the Grand Prix du Roman from the Académie Française for his most recent novel, *Les Onze* (The Eleven), and the Prix de la Ville de Paris for his entire opus.

In *Rimbaud le fils*, Michon asks what drives art. What explains a poet's devotion to the word and then our own devotion to that poet after he abandons it? Through Rimbaud, Michon explores his recurring themes: the absent father, the smothering mother, the backwater upbringing, and how they shape that tortured mix of genius and ambition we call an artist. Although

Michon begins with Vitalie Cuif, Rimbaud's mother, it is really the paternal line, the father—or fathers—that interests him. *Rimbaud le fils* traces lineage as determined by literature and how Rimbaud becomes literature incarnate, only to reject that patrimony.

Michon is a virtuosic writer whose medium is language, yet his imagination is visual. Rimbaud is revealed to us in images. We see him first sitting for a school photograph. Later we follow him to Étienne Carjat's studio for the shooting of that iconic portrait with the crooked tie. And finally there he is in Harar, posing before the banana fields, a figure no longer identifiable as "poetry in person." These are all photographs but Michon's methods are painterly. His eye for color, his sense of depth, dimension, composition, the way he returns again and again to the image, adding layer upon layer—all this renders *Rimbaud le fils* a meticulously painted canvas, or many canvases, from which the poet eternally escapes.

Dense and poetic, Michon's work calls for every translation trick in the book. A Michon sentence is an architectural feat: shift the position of a verb, extract a semicolon, and the whole thing topples. But the delight of bringing Michon into English is multiplied by the daunting nature of the task. And by the sheer mastery of Michon's prose: "What makes men write? Other men, their mothers, the stars, or the old enormous things, God, language? The powers know. The powers of the air are this breath of wind through the leaves. The night turns. The moon rises, there is no one against the haystack. Rimbaud, in the attic among some pages, has turned toward the wall and sleeps like lead." What makes men write? Michon does not answer this question. But few writers have asked it so beautifully.

Rimbaud
the Son

IT IS SAID THAT VITALIE RIMBAUD, NÉE CUIF

It is said that Vitalie Rimbaud, née Cuif, country girl and
bad-natured woman, suffering and bad-natured, gave birth to
Arthur Rimbaud. It is not known if she cursed first and suffered
after, or if she cursed at having to suffer and persisted in that
malediction; or if, joined like the fingers on her hand, curse and
suffering overlapped in her mind, switched places, reinforced
one another, so that, irritated by their touch, she crushed her
life, her son, her living and her dead between her dark fingers.
But it is known that the husband of this woman who was the
father of this son, although alive, became a phantom in the
purgatory of distant garrisons where he was only a name, when
the son was six years old. There is some debate over whether that
lightweight father, who was a captain, who read Arabic and
dabbled in the annotation of grammar books, was justified in
abandoning that creature of darkness who wanted to sweep him
under her shadow, or if she only became that way because of the
darkness into which his departure cast her; we just do not know.
It is said that the child, with phantom on one side of his desk
and creature of curse and disaster on the other, was the perfect
schoolboy and had a strong attraction for the ancient game of
verse: perhaps in the old perfunctory tempo of twelve feet he

heard the phantom bugle of distant garrisons, and also the paternosters of the creature of disaster who, in order to recite her
accursed suffering, had found God, just as her son, to the same
end, discovered verse; and in that scansion he married the bugle
and the paternosters, perfectly. Verse is an old matchmaker. So
it seems that he composed it in great quantities from a very
tender age, some in Latin, some in French; in these verses,
which still exist, no miracle took place: they are from the hand
of a gifted provincial child whose anger has not yet found its
own consubstantial rhythm, that true rhythm thanks to which it
is changed into charity without losing a fraction of its fine edge,
anger and charity blended in the same movement released in a
single burst and falling back with all their weight, or taking off
but remaining there mixed, heavy, disabled, like fireworks that
go off in your hand though sparking impeccably, all of which
would later assume the name of Arthur Rimbaud. These were
the exercises of a schoolboy. In the period when he was covering
page after lined page with these practice scales, it is clear that
the polite smile was not his forte and that he sulked, as shown in
the photos that devout hands here and there have collected,
multiplied like loaves, and that have passed unaltered through
all the devout hands in the world: with, on his lap, the small
round military cap of the Rossat Institute in Charleville, with
that ridiculous scrap of clerical lingerie on his arm with which
mothers used to deck out their sons for communion, here his
small fingers slipped into the edge of a missal that appears cab-

bage green, there well hidden in the secret hollow of the kepi, but always the direct and wicked gaze, held out before him like a fist, as though greatly detesting or desiring the photographer who in those days covered himself with a black hood in order to fashion a future out of the past, to tamper with time, the child endlessly sulked. And the rest of his life, or our devotion, teaches us that beneath that appearance the true extent of his anger was considerable: not simply against the armband and the kepi but against the armband and the kepi as well. For under those old castoffs, it is said, there was the shade of the Captain and the living creature of refusal and disaster, of refusal in the name of God who castigated his soul in order that he become Rimbaud: not there in person, but their fabled effigies on either side of the desk; and though perhaps hating them both with all his might, and thus hating the verses in which paternosters and bugles married, he truly loved the mission that they required of him. That was why he was sulking. He persisted, and we know what followed.

Or perhaps he did not hate them at all: hate is not a good matchmaker. Verses are made to be given away, so that in exchange you are given something resembling love; they compose bridal wreaths; and as disastrous as she was, perhaps because she was so, the creature's vocation more than anyone's was to receive love, and why not give it: like everyone else, she aspired to impossible nuptials, whether knowingly or not. But since she had foundered in paternosters, had devoted herself to the dark, to the dark fingers inside her ripping her joy to shreds, since she had gotten herself up to her neck in the irremediable, the incommensurable, and finally since she, too, sulked, the usual childish gifts, the flowers and little smiles, the Hugoesque sentimentalities, which are, after all, part of reality as well and keep love circulating among creatures without disaster, all that was lost on her. The flowers and little smiles she ripped to shreds, like everything else: because she did not love this son who was her, because she did not love herself, who knows? because all she loved in herself was the bottomless well in which everything foundered; and she was too busy feeling her way along the dark walls of that well, groping for the bottom, to notice the small flowers that grew on the coping. More potent offerings were needed. And the son, having always known that the bouquets and simpering smiles, the neat tie, clean trousers, the air of the little gentleman, all filial artifices reminiscent of Victor Hugo were not sufficient, did not work, were rejected, fell into the well, crushed between two dark fingers, her son had found a solution equal to her own, and fashioned for that incommensurable grief incommensurable little gifts—paternosters of his own invention: long passages of rhymed language that she did not understand, but as she pored over them perhaps without being able to read them she saw something disproportionate as her well and unrelenting as her fingers, the mark of a ravaging passion that has forgotten its cause and overshot its effect, of pure, ineffectual love; churchlike things wrapped up in lugubrious finales, smacking of the boot and the dungeon; wooden language out of which he made her a gift box; Latin diatribes on Jugurtha and Hercules, dead captains of the dead language; and in those diatribes no doubt there were flights of doves, June mornings and trumpets, but it all fell onto the page in an opaque idiom of pure December, arranged calligraphically as verses are, that is to say, between two margins a sheer, narrow well of ink, to the bottom of which you drop, page after page. And before all that perhaps she exulted, wordlessly; she recognized herself, and in the Charleville dining room the seated child who looked up at her saw her gaping for a moment, as if astonished, respectful, envious, the fingers in her ceasing to crush the dark and the source of curse drying up, growing calm, as if in this wooden language that she could not read she sensed the work of a well digger more powerful than she was, who dug more deeply and more irremediably, who was her master and in some way her savior. It could be that she caressed his head then. Because it was a gift, in a sense. And when at other times the child read aloud before her the final draft of his Virgilian verses honed to their most true for the local competition, as we can imagine he often did, just as the girls at Saint-Cyr did for the king, and she, the country girl, seated like the king, flabbergasted but reticent, disdainful, royal, which is to say merciless, when thus he went before her with his most high paternosters, he, too, royal, impassioned, admirable and ridiculous like the little Bonaparte at Brienne, vaguely terrifying like him, we can imagine that they were closer at that time than they would have thought possible; but very far apart, both of them on their thrones and not wanting to come down, in the way of two sovereigns of distant capitals who are in correspondence. So in his early years he spoke his poetry and she listened, I am sure. They gave each other this gift, as others offer bouquets and are then embraced by their mothers, under the smiling gaze of their fathers; and the father was there as well, they could hear the lost bugle in the wooden language. Yes, those two incommensurables face to face in Charleville dining rooms crossed swords with one another, gave each other a kind of love: did so by means of language suspended in the air and rhythmical. But while the language conducted its sabbath high above the dining-room light, they themselves, their bodies here below, seated, or standing and reciting leaning against the table, their bodies sulked.

And that too has no doubt been said, because with regard to that childish pout before the photographer, and with regard to Vitalie Rimbaud's pout which is not known because no photographer captured it once and for all under his black hood, everything has been said. And nearly everything has been said as well with regard to the other one who must not have been very much fun either, the shade who attended those verbal jousts in the dining room in absentia, the Captain, of whom for now we have no photograph either, and yet sometimes we have no doubt that he posed in Purgatory before a camera, among some noncommissioned officers in distant garrisons, smoothing his imperial beard with two fingers or playing cards or with his hand on his sword—and maybe at the precise moment when he remembered young Arthur. He remembers Arthur in a garret in the Ardennes, in yellowed sepia; it is a hundred years since anyone has seen him, behind him a bugle sounds, we do not hear it. The devout will find this portrait some day, you will muse over it, you will see the hand on the hilt or smoothing the moustache, you will not know what he was thinking. But for the moment you do not know this face.

On the other hand, we know the faces of the child's other relatives because there are photographs of them, and before photographs, painted portraits, from the age when only the hand of the painter tampered with time, using pigments from the earth, not yet the silver chlorides in the box of tricks under the black hood. Because as we know, other ancestors engendered him, remained close to him, not only in photographs, and they were as much at his beck and call as the mother was intractable, and less phantoms on the whole than the father, more flagrant, better vouched for by the thick books with their names on them than the father with his Bescherelle grammar book, abandoned in Charleville in the haste of his departure, which was also thick, it is true, but the trace of the father in the margins, learned annotations in spidery scrawl, was infinitesimal; and the grammar book did not bear the name of Rimbaud printed on it, but the name of the Bescherelle brothers. Yes, pure of any kinship with the Captain and the Captain's wife, and perhaps also contingent with regard to them as the seven distant planets are with regard to the moon and the sun, the grandfathers appeared magisterially, the beacons as they were called, distant stars in the darkness of schools, Malherbe and

Racine, Hugo, Baudelaire and little Banville; who, one arising from the next, had begotten one another in approximately that order, had launched the canonical filiation that heats up the twelve feet two by two, all come from there, all strung along the great twelve-foot rod like brilliant diverse but similar rings, and out of that slight variation being born, being named; who, by that very long umbilical cord stretching back to Virgil, Virgil who had not needed twelve feet because he was the Old Man, the founder, he had all license; who, beyond Virgil, beyond Homer, were rooted perhaps in the heart of the ineffable Name; who, to perpetuate the lineage, all had special license from beyond to beget one another, bypassing women, bypassing the cursing women, and speaking louder than the cursing women, in big mute books; and the latest offspring had this pile of readily available ancestors on his little desk in Charleville. He was not sure that he would be among them; but he already was, because as loyally as he venerated them, he did not only venerate them, he detested them in that same heart; they stood between him and the ineffable Name, they were heavy, they were in the way. We know that he surpassed them in the end, that he vanquished them and was their master; in no time at all, he broke the rod and on it broke himself.

2

AND AMONG ALL THOSE AWARDS DAY FIGURES

And among all those Awards Day figures, the seventeenth-
century wigs, the beards of 1830, Racine, Hugo, the others,
whose busts at that time sat on pianos, behind large bouquets of
peonies in the homes of genteel nightcaps who believed themselves to be poets and who were, or perhaps whose small, two-bit
lithographs decorated the garrets of young greenhorn poseurs
who believed themselves to be poets and who were, among all
those bronze and wooden faces appears for us the poet Georges
Izambard, famous in his way. Only the muse duped him, so he
does not rise among the stars in the procession of the masters of
the rod, no one made a bust of him, he is in the abyss where the
twelve syllables let him fall. He dedicated his life to them. The
rod loves whom it pleases. He too wanted to be Shakespeare, in
his youth: but that came to an end when he was twenty-two
years old, in the spring of 1870, in that schoolroom by the window through which schoolboys saw chestnut trees in blossom,
and where he alone, Izambard, saw Rimbaud on a school bench
become Rimbaud. The poet Izambard holds for eternity the
Charleville School chair in rhetoric; he is forever twenty-two
years old, his long life a dead letter, and as for the collections
that he nevertheless composed and later published, in the eyes

of time it is as though he had pissed into the wind. But he was
that young man in that classroom; that is why his photograph is
there, not very large, not full-page, at the very beginning of the
iconographies, as some vague precursor or minor figure could
have appeared if photography had been invented at the time of
the ancient referential story, a second, not even John the Baptist,
not even Joseph the carpenter, but maybe the head workman in
Joseph's shop, the one who taught the Son how to hold a plane
and whom the four Gospels do not even mention. And of course
in this case the plane was the twelve feet in the French style,
with all their old tricks since Malherbe, with all their new tricks
too, those of the good Parnassians invoked by Izambard. Conse-
quently, beginning with Izambard, the schoolboy's practice
scales abandoned the wooden language of the *oremus* and easily
played the hereditary instrument, the one passed down from
Villon to Coppée; that is, French; where meaning openly appears: from then on he could have dedicated his diatribes to the
queen Carabosse in the same language that Carabosse spoke,
and no longer in the matte idiom of December, he could have
pitted himself against her in the language of June. But he did
not do so; apparently those diatribes were no longer for her:
because he was a grown boy now and had let go of his mother's
skirts; above all because if he had spoken those verses under the
dining-room light, his love would have burst forth without measure in the clarity of the meaning, and he would have fallen on
the floor before her, babbling like an infant, his infant tears
rendering him speechless from the first hemistich, and perhaps

then in the clarity of the meaning she would have passionately picked him up, sat him on her knees, wiped his nose, caressed him and consoled him; perhaps she herself would have been a bit consoled: and poetry does not want such consolations, they render it mute. It is also said that under Izambard's reign, right beneath his eyes the practice scales became a work of art, that is to say an ogre; and if the child did not deign to recite them to the old queen it was because his anger toward her had grown, was hungry, felt its wings and seven-league boots, burned to pit itself against sovereigns of another caliber, to bring them down one after another, mercilessly to dig wells under them to engulf them. And he began with Izambard.

Nevertheless he loved Izambard; but the work, the art, made use of Izambard and did not love him.

No doubt the creature of disaster knew that and could not say it, but not Izambard, who could have said it; not Izambard, fresh from teachers college with his gentle air and his cocky ways, his little pince-nez, the quiver of his lip, his hair slightly but not overly long, that fervent republicanism that his whole figure bore, that reserve, decent, timid and brave, which is how he remains, behind the silver chlorides with which the great magic captured him at twenty-two years old. Alas, the poet Izambard knew nothing of all that when he began his school year in 1870, crossed the courtyard under the chestnut trees, caught sight of the little group in caps who were waiting for him there outside the classroom, and straightened up cockily then, nose in the air toward the clear sky and fashioning for himself who knows what azure—an azure without malice in any case: because, out of bravery or timidity, he did not want to see the pall that is behind perfect azures, is basic and fundamental to them, and which it is precisely azure's mission to conceal, to paint in glory; without which azure is a pot of blue paint, a lapis-lazuli preciosity; and he loved and practiced poetry no doubt, but in the way of those men passionate about hunting, books on hunting, the lovely stories of autumn with feathers and blood, high-sounding words of venery, of falconry, hunting horns in a corner of the woods resounding like an angel, but who, gun in hand and hare with its expressive ears bolting at their feet, begin to tremble, close their eyes and shoot to the side. And when they return they say that it was a good hunt. Neither did Izambard want to kill anyone and nevertheless believed that it would be a good hunt; and if, entering his classroom after lessons and taking a seat at his request, you had asked him what he considered poetry to be, he no doubt would have responded, blushing, becoming flustered, perhaps removing his pince-nez to wipe the condensation with a teachers college handkerchief, and gazing out the window rather than looking at you, he would have answered in a tone of both audacity and panic that it was a matter of the heart thanks to which language is adorned like a bride, or perhaps since Baudelaire, eyes made up, pockmarked, but glorious and adorned like a fine whore—but surely not a dark peasant woman who digs a hole into which language disproportionately plunges and vibrates. He believed that it *was good*, poetry; that it was entirely on the side of good, the Republic and Awards Day, and

not on the side of Sedan and great massacres; that it was one's
duty to remove the obstacles spitefully placed before poetry by
evil spirits, which lead to deaths and above all to those invita-
tions to crime, the armband and the kepi: and that, with those
garish rags stripped away, each of us would democratically become a poet, because it only takes a childlike imagination, the
discipline of rhymes and the freedom of freedom. You would
have granted him the discipline of rhymes; as for the rest, no
doubt you would have had your reservations and kept them to
yourself; but if you found yourself impassioned by this young
man's impromptu speech, your legs stretched uncomfortably
under the small desk and your heart nevertheless exalted by the
high blossoms in the leaves almost discernible through the window, if thus you had objected that poetry cannot be wholly on
the side of good, since our first parents in the Garden of Eden
did not speak, communicated in the way of flowers through
bees, winged messengers, and would feel their tongues loosen
only after the angel had shown them the door; if you had argued
that language comes to humans after the Fall, when matter no
longer sings; that poetry, which is the language of language, also
falls into the universal well and perhaps twice as quickly, unless
in its frenzied duplication it ceaselessly climbs back up using all
its strength, is almost at the coping, falls back deeper, and so
makes use of its free freedom—and if you yourself were indecisive then, searching for words, blurting them out with audacity
and panic—then he would have carefully folded the teachers
college handkerchief, replaced his pince-nez, and looking you

up and down, clearing his throat, would have asked you coldly
to which sect you belonged. And you would have blushed in
turn, gazed out at the chestnut trees in the evening, and spoken
of Sedan.

Although it would not have been Sedan that crossed your
lips; you are in that classroom three to six months before Sedan,
before Sedan becomes that closed fist in history, when it is still
only a garrison in the Ardennes; you would have spoken of
Solferino or Sebastopol, some massacre or another, only to em-
phasize that evil is out there, not in Malherbe but in Louis-
Napoleon, not in language but in the aberration of action, flagrant and indisputable when the Carabosse of combat, the god-
dess of crows, is dancing on dead armies; and to agree heartily
with Izambard that the Carabosses are in the armband and the
kepi, but not in poetry, which is all good fairy. And Izambard,
reassured—not about poetry but on your account—would have
accompanied you to the door, said his polite teachers college
good-byes, made a Latin joke; and you would have taken leave
of him with a Latin joke and much inward respect; because
Izambard was one of those men thanks to whom the world can
endure, for whom evil is elsewhere, close at hand but outside,
omnipresent but remediable, one of that old species of men who
fight for the good that they believe they feel inside themselves:
and since at twenty-two he thought that Carabosse—I mean
Vitalie Cuif this time—was exactly the opposite of poetry, that
she was an obstacle in its way, that she was guilty of too much
prose and of corrupting the free poetry of her son, he helped

Arthur to rid himself of her; and for the future of *la poésie française*, if that old nightingale still exists, he did well—but not in the way he believed he did well: because as often happens, the mother, dismissed from the affections of the son, repudiated, mocked, excluded from the world and disavowed, the mother disappeared from among the visible creatures and took refuge completely within the son, gathered her old skirts in both hands and leapt wholly into the son, into that dark, never-opened inner closet where, we are told, we are unconscious of our actions and we act; there she rejoined the Captain, who had been there for some time with his sword and his shako; but she made more noise than the Captain. And such things often happen; but it happens less often that the son is Arthur Rimbaud, whose notable actions were only beautiful verses; and it was with the dark fingers that I mentioned, but this time tampering with the son, gripping the son, locked into the son, that the most beautiful verses were spun out two by two: yes, we can imagine that the age-old alexandrine was prodigiously exalted, then irrevocably destroyed in about 1872 by a sad woman who scratched, flailed and raved in a child.

Perhaps after all Izambard had an inkling of that, though it was beyond him. Perhaps when, a year later, Rimbaud mocked and disposed of him in his turn, sold off the good master's books and put him in the closet, he discerned that poetry *was bad*; that the old witch whom he believed he was doing in was, in the end, the one who made poetry and would do him in; he could not not perceive all that, anymore than he could admit that he had perceived it: and that is undoubtedly why, knowing but not wanting to know, the poet Izambard forever pissed into the wind. And that is not our concern. We can leave that classroom; put on your top hat, there are boys watching you: they raise their little shakos when you pass them in the shade of the chestnut trees, they take you for the inspector, perhaps one of them is scowling, sticks up his nose conspicuously and keeps his kepi firmly on. Nothing is more beautiful than those May chestnut trees above him. Remaining at his doorway, the rhetoric class-room already dark behind him, Izambard regards the evening shadow and you, leaving, within it, you become that shadow. He is talking to himself in Latin. You did not turn around; what you are seeking is not within Izambard's domain.

3

NEITHER WAS IT WITHIN BANVILLE'S DOMAIN

Neither was it within Banville's domain.

He too appears in this story, not long after Izambard, because we know that the adolescent sent him verses, care of the
publisher Lemerre, into which he had put his whole heart; and
the first, no doubt, that he considered presentable to an established poet. The triumphs of Awards Day were no longer
enough for him; they had served their purpose; they had nur-
tured in that angry heart a brutal ambition at the same time as
was born there that uncertain faculty, pose or task or revelation
from On High, or a bit of all three, that was called *genius* in
those times, that almost supernatural attribute that never appears itself, overhead or in the living visible body, as halo, vigor,
beauty, or youth, but that nevertheless appears in minute effects
and which is confirmed in the perfection of bits of coded language more or less lengthy written in black and white. We know
that these bits are generally infinitesimal. We who read them
never know if they are perfect or if it was whispered to us in
childhood that they were perfect, and we in turn whisper it to
others, ad infinitum; and the one who writes them does not
know any more than we do, if anything less, he knows it only at
the moment when he joins the rods, when fitting together flaw-

lessly like mortise and tenon they briefly exult, closing with the triumphant sound of jaws, and it is over; and when it is over once again he trembles, that is him, the poet, in those jaws, the rod has deserted him there and he no longer knows how to write, even if he, like Field Marshal Hugo, had laid out rod upon rod until he died, even if he himself were the jubilant jaws of the shark and *verse in person*. Thus he trembles at his desk like a rat; but when he goes out he wants some kind of halo to appear over his head, and he wants to be told so: for he cannot see it himself. And to return to Rimbaud's genius, to that most precise and furious ambition in the heart of the Ardennes in the scrap of a sulky man who was also and at the same time pure love—because all that is mixed together, byzantine and multiple as the old theology—to return to the one who is like the emblem for that conflict, that byzantine knot, we do not know if ambition precedes or foments genius, engenders it by strength of toil, or if, on the contrary, by pure miracle unfurling its wings, genius only afterward becomes aware of the shadow they cast and the men who rush into this mirage, and from then on, he who is the plaything of that phantom attribute and projects that shadow becomes infatuated with it, wants ever more of it, damns himself.

No, we do not know if it is pure or impure. We do not know if at the beginning there is the Word or the stack of ribboned books that, with little ceremonies, a subprefect in full uniform on a raised platform delivers into your hands. But, born of the Word, which since the beginning whispers where it will and has no residence, not Charleville, Patmos, or Guernsey, or born very locally of awards in excellence acclaimed in a local school auditorium in July with potted plants and flags, there is *genius*, since the word is in the language; since we use this abuse of language; and no doubt it does not exist, but the poets of that time wanted to be rewarded with that which did not exist: the older ones wanted to be reassured continually by honorary chairs under the dome of the Academy, by crowds taking off their hats to them, and when through misfortune they were without an audience in Guernsey, they summoned out of the air Shakespeare, Mozart, Virgil, who in fatherly fashion rushed over the sea to reassure them, with all the little hands of the sea clapping—and in heavy weather the big hands: and the Old Man on his gray island leaning over his séance table was at the opening night of *Hernani* with the red waistcoat, exiled he heard the audience of *Hernani*. And the young ones waited for the old ones out of courtesy and reciprocity, perhaps belief mitigated by augury between them, a great fear of augury suspended between men and gods, who are both fearsome, the young ones waited for the recognized poets, that is, the ones whose names had at least once in some context brushed up against the word *genius*, for those poets to grant them a small ray from that invisible halo that they were reputed to have over their heads; and which is transmitted as if by cuttings, from the oldest to the youngest, but that the young can never quite steal, not even Rimbaud or Saint John, the old must proffer it: and it was of Banville that Rimbaud asked that immense small favor.

We no longer hear of Banville, he too pissed into the wind; and he did not even enjoy the combined benefits of mystery and failure, of the loss of being, that Izambard's shade enjoyed. If we go by the anthology pieces (since no one bothers to read the complete versions anymore, except perhaps some old auto-didact, a Léautaud from Douai or Confolens who, leaving the library, curses the Walkmen and the motorbikes, or more op-timistically, a very young country girl who climbed up to the attic in June, when school is closed and the heart wide open to the infinite freedom of objectless loves, and in the attic she found among old dresses *Les Cariatides* by Théodore de Ban-ville, an old book of poems that she reads alone under the linden tree until dark), if we can go by those pieces, always the same ones, which must indeed be the best of them but which seem so poor, Banville was not a brilliant poet—at least he no longer seems so to us—and yet in his lifetime he seemed so: someone is mistaken in this matter, Baudelaire or you, me or Sainte-Beuve, Rimbaud or the descendants of Rimbaud, who knows? men of letters are futile. We have not read his verses, except for those eternal trifles from selected pieces with their Bacchuses that in the corner of the woods our grandmothers might take for slightly tipsy grandsons, and their violet-eyed erect young Athenian girls, pretty in their way, but with so little ass under their tunics. We have not read him. But we know, because we have read about him, that he too was prodigiously precocious, from his infancy possessed great ambition and pure love, the seven-league boots, came from Moulins as Bonaparte

from Ajaccio and Rimbaud from Charleville with a strong will
to be done with old-fashioned poetry, and proudly launched
those *Cariatides* in Paris, which, says Baudelaire, no one would
believe a young fellow of eighteen to have written. Yes, we know
that Baudelaire held him in high esteem and was his friend, that
he set him apart as he did Chateaubriand and Flaubert, above
the modern riffraff as he put it, which perhaps distinguishes
him, unless it was polite augury; we know that for a long time he
slept with the fat Marie Daubrun, whom Baudelaire so desired;
that they had a falling out over her and that much later the
munificent Banville, a decent man, sent a petition to the minis-
ter so that the poor human wreck of Brussels could draw a
pension, have his clothes brushed, his old man's food brought
to his imbecile mouth by an almost friendly hand, perhaps
glimpse a skirt, chant his *crénom* without a thought for tomorrow. And that distinguishes him. Furthermore, from Gide's slan-
der we know that the affability of his criticism was such that,
reading it, one would think one was eating jam; from Doctor
Mondor we know that he highly prized and revived the little
forms fallen into female hands: the rondeau, double rondeau,
lay, virelay, villanelle, chant royal; from Mallarmé that he *was
not somebody special, but the very sound of the lyre*; and that this
somebody who was in the end nobody, as a good bourgeois, as a
good poet, loved to walk in the Luxembourg Gardens *dear to the
passerby*, and from there under the leaves certainly eyed the
dome of the Pantheon close by, believing, not believing, that he
had laid enough rods two by two to be laid himself in return one

day there below in the shade of the vault that is to the great dead what the June leaves are to the passersby; and of course that is also why, because of that finally modest ambition, he was not Rimbaud; but that is not the only reason. We also know about his voice, from Antonin Proust, who heard it, from the time when it rang forth into the day: it was musical, lilting, a bit high and fluty, like Mallarmé's; in that high-perched voice he liked to proclaim: *I am a lyric poet and make my living from it*—and we can well imagine all of that together, the fluty voice, the bland affirmation, half sincere, half silly, and beneath it all a bit of specious ferocity, the Louis-Philippardian stroll to the Luxembourg, gaze drawn toward the dome: Banville is a type that we have all encountered a hundred times. Finally, from Verlaine we have the precious knowledge that he strikingly resembled Watteau's Gilles, so that he could have been taken for him had this Gilles happened to be strolling in Paris—that he thus resembled Charles Carreau, parish priest of Nogent-sur-Marne and Watteau's model, and there was no danger of mistaking them for one another because, since 1721, the model no longer set foot in the Luxembourg or anywhere else, and was under the marly earth of the Marne. Banville had the Gilles's reddened nose and his dazed look of a boy about to cry, perhaps his very old soul; and the silver chlorides, obediently reproducing as is their custom, photo after photo perfectly identical in the way of amoebas, in my case perfectly reproduced on page 39 of the Rimbaud iconography that lies open before me, the silver chlorides are in agreement with Verlaine on this point.

Watteau's Gilles wrote neoclassical nonsense; at least that is
what is said of him today. But if in those times you had been a
poet, a young poet, not quite Rimbaud of course but almost, if
you too were tired of old-fashioned poetics, you would have
turned the corner of boulevard Saint-Germain, heart pounding,
into rue de Buci, where Banville lived; with his letter of encour-
agement in your pocket, which you had received in Douai or
Confolens, affable as jam. You would have seen your hand
tremble as it pushed open the carriage entrance of 10, rue de
Buci; and in the depths of the cool, dark inner courtyard, filled
with the sounds of the city though they seemed distant, like
phantoms, you would have hesitated for a long time. You hesitate; you look up into the air, the mute windows of a *great poet*,
and above the windows the month of June; because it is June,
the four feet of that blue throne resting on the roofs. And at the
same time as June, it is the evidence of poetic inanity that hits
you; that is sitting on you, under which you are gasping for
breath: because of course compared to June your pieces regarding June are pitiful; and without even considering June, which
is very high and rebellious like Meaning, just considering language, the little corrupted code, the meager but inexhaustible
hand with which meaning is made, not even meaning, the
game of meaning, which has the air of a meaning, even compared to that, your poems hardly measure up; and your verses
are far from true, powerless to translate what you are, the suffering void that you are, into pure prayer without waste. Into the
language of June. No, nothing triumphs disproportionately in

the poem, not June, not language, not you. So you flee, you are already at the gare d'Austerlitz, the evening trains are so beautiful when one is rid of the burden of having to speak about them.

But perhaps in that courtyard you do not flee: in June above a sparrow passes; you murmur for yourself alone one of those verses that are called perfect because they note the impossibility of recording all at once June, one's own distress, and the whole of language, but which stand their ground in that impossibility, and standing, play the trumpet; this is Baudelaire; one or the other, the sparrow or Baudelaire, whispers to you that the imposture, poetic inanity, is also a kind of courage. You forgive yourself. And you also forgive Banville, who is only a man, for having definitively opted for language for want of June, for having buried himself within it, and there within having become *the very sound of the lyre*, that is to say, nobody. The lyre is no cause for fear, only men are: you climb the stairs with all the strength of your young legs, and you ring Théodore de Banville's doorbell.

(And of course there I could see you both, on either side of the large bouquet, peonies or hydrangeas, there on the poet's desk: the floured one, who is at the same time the ineffable sound, and you. You would not have said that you have come for the little cutting, the one that is transmitted from the oldest to the youngest, the little cutting of genius, that is to say, permission to eat at the poetic trough or to spit in it, the entrance pass to the domes, Guernsey or Harar, it is up to you; and he would not have said that he was on the point of giving it to you: because that is done without saying so, while speaking of something else.

You speak of those things, I hear you; and Banville's perched voice perches higher as he extols the form, the truth that inheres in syntax more than in our desires, in rhyme more than in our hearts—the thousand inanities of the hedonism of literature, the *Enlightenment* pose, the pose of the mind—and you, half hidden behind that large bouquet of peonies, I could see you turn red as the flowers, gritting your teeth, keeping to yourself and chewing over the fable of Meaning, of salvation through language, of God who wants to appear in it and who cannot because of Banville and his kind—the thousand inanities of the idealism of literature, the *red waistcoat* pose, the pose of the heart; or, on the contrary, to please Banville, to conform to what he expects of your eighteen years, there you are getting up on your high horse, letting loose on him a whole tirade, you take the pose of the heart one step farther; and there is so much of youth in your insolence that you feel the Confolens suit ripping across your shoulders from the pressure of wings; and the munificent Banville pretends to see those wings. He smiles. He tells you that you remind him of Boyer or Baudelaire when they were twenty; and at those words you know that over the bouquet of peonies he has just invisibly offered you the little cutting, and without even getting up you have taken it, it is in your pocket.

What calm within you then, what power, what a glorious future: but you are not Arthur Rimbaud.)

4

THAT POET, WHO NO LONGER CASTS A SHADOW

That poet, who no longer casts a shadow, thus received two letters from the very young Rimbaud, who casts upon us as great a shadow as Dante's little bonnet casts upon the Italian language and Virgil's laurels cast upon Dante—because men of letters are futile, timid, devout. Reading them, Banville sensed his Julien Sorel of the Ardennes at fifty leagues; and in that he was not mistaken: letters are little traps for others, just one other, whom one wants to put in one's pocket; and Rimbaud excelled in this discipline of bird-catching. Verses are greater traps for more ineffable prey. And in the verses that went with those letters, that were the basis and justification for them, Banville surely heard something altogether different, different from Rastignac or Sorel, because for all that Banville was, that is to say nightingale and nightcap, the uninterrupted attention required by the Dome yonder, he knew how to make two verses hold together, and, which is something else again, how, in the pincer of two verses, to hold a little of the world; he had done that all his life. Under the gifted, clever, Hugoesque young versifier, under the flagrant rhymes, Banville heard the other, darker rhyme, unknown to the rhymer, that could not care less about the one in whom it sings, or squeaks; which is born of the very

ancient way each of us knots together June, language, and ourselves—and in some that makes music: a thin stave of three or
four notes, but tyrannical, tyrannically reiterated and combined,
the variety of its combinations making great poets, as they are
called; and that stave, that song, that tyranny muddles the
rhymer's plans and decides from start to finish for him: perhaps
that is what decides that you wake up as Julien Sorel, that mid-
way through your life you compose a small thing as unassailable
and laughable as Dante's bonnet (meanwhile that small thing is
published, you call it *Les Fleurs du mal*, it is only a tiny mile-
stone in the conquest of Paris), that all afternoon you spend
waiting in vain for that small thing to make you king, and,
without knowing how it happened, that you mutter a single
terrifying *crénom* one evening in a cheap joint in Brussels; and
when finally you go to bed you still believe that you are Julien
Sorel, but at the end of the line; until you are a corpse you
believe it, even though you have written *Les Fleurs du mal*. And
at least once Banville had encountered in flesh and blood that
aberrant ambition that makes great poets, from it he had even
stolen the fat Marie Daubrun, for it he had petitioned the minis-
ter for a pauper's pension; and he knew how to recognize it.
Thus he recognized it in Rimbaud's verses. That is what we
want to believe, since we are devout; but sometimes we have
doubts; and when we have doubts we tell ourselves that its
music is not so obvious, that perhaps by dint of paternosters we
are the ones who put it there, not God, not all the muses assembled at Charleville, not *genius*; that a century of devotion to

these staves is solely responsible for the notes. No matter, that is how things stand: perhaps it is only a little ditty, but it resounds fantastically in us like the great organ swells of a *Te Deum*.

Devoutly we want to believe that Banville heard the *Te Deum*; that perhaps he heard in the schoolboy's verse a very distant echo of the leap that Carabosse made into the inner closet; her marriage with the Captain renewed there; the perfect nuptials of bugle and paternosters; the ridiculous little domestic drama magnified into a high mass, set forth in clear language, but draped, unrecognizable. Or if you prefer quainter images, borrowed from the catechism of that time, which Banville read, and not from those family histories which are our own meager catechism, the obscure rhyme that he heard was the one that strikes charity and anger against one another, infinite rancor and mercy, holds them in each hand, each of them distinct, intact, irreconcilable, sworn enemies, and releases one against the other like fighting cocks, unleashes them, recaptures them, and punctuates that explosion with a great confrontation of drums. And if your personal devotion offers you other metaphors (which you take for thought and which are thought), you call the two terms of this little tom-tom by different names: you say that it is revolt and pure love, or nothingness and salvation, or the endless fall and within the fall the inexhaustible presence of what is no longer called God; you say that it is in mourning God and in pretending God is restored; and if you do not like God you say that it is the free joy of being alive and the darker joy of being slave to death, whatever: what matters is having the great cymbals well in hand, knowing how to make them clash and that they make that noise one hears in Rimbaud. And lending an ear to that music, Banville, who was not dishonest, who had long ago lost that inner rhyme but knew how to recognize it in others, Banville picked up a pen thoughtfully and prepared to reply; in silk skullcap at his poet's desk, with the peonies and no doubt some Doric knick-knack close at hand that served as paperweight, pensively stirring the tea with rum that Verlaine tells us one drank at his house, reflecting, weighing the pros and the cons, this man who resembled the Gilles replied. He paid the young man from the Ardennes the courtesy of augury, and sent by post the little cutting in letters that are no longer in our possession.

Perhaps I am wasting my time with Banville. I am wasting my time with this poor old man who yesterday came from Moulins with all the poetry of the earth in his heart and who is being destroyed in Paris by schemes, success, power and the approach of death; Banville, whose only function is to be interim leading poet—because Hugo on his island is unavailable, bent over he listens to the beat of Shakespeare's foot in the four feet of his table—that is to say, to deliver the little cutting to the greenhorns of Douai or Charleville; Banville who is nothing, hardly the shadow that returning down rue de Rome lifts his head toward the pigeons on the dome. Nevertheless, I still want to repeat how precious it is to me that this poor man resembles, to the point of being mistaken for, Watteau's Gilles.

Thus it is the Gilles who opens the dance of Rimbaud's

readers. It is precious to me that he was the first (the first in Paris
of course, Charleville does not count in these matters) who,
bent over that poet's desk where he is catching up on correspon-
dences, reads the verses of the white blackbird from Charleville;
and that he replies; that he adds words to those words; that thus
he is also the first to make comments, in terms we do not know,
for the benefit of the author of those verses he has read closely—
and for a hundred years his shadow is yoked to that letter, like
those dolts in stories whom mischievous fate tethers to an iniq-
uitous and monotonous task, he has not moved from that desk,
he is replying to Rimbaud. Interminably he returns to the letter.
His conviction has waned, but the fairy wants him to continue: a
dark fairy who is inside that small mixture of work and life we
call Rimbaud, and who transforms those who approach him
into Banville, into Pierrot. Because it may be that all the books
now written on Rimbaud, the one I am writing and those that
will be written tomorrow, were written, are written, and will be
written by Théodore de Banville—not exactly by Banville, not
all of them, but all without exception by Watteau's Gilles. Some
are very much the work of a man we can call Banville, as Banville in person: by the countless Banvilles, that is to say, by a
nearly perfect, well-meaning man of poetry, upright, timid but
well-meaning, a poseur but sincere, hotheaded, a bit of a nightingale, a bit old-fashioned even if he is very young, and tousled
or neatly combed according to inclination, the tousled ones
stand for anger and nothingness, the neatly combed for salvation
and charity, but they always lack the other cymbal; or there are

two cymbals, but not at the same time; and if they were tousled
when they were young, there they are in old age in the Luxembourg Gardens airing their white manes beneath the foliage,
they, too, are eyeing the dome of the Pantheon, or less visible
paradises, the gold of Time, the magnetic field of the beyond,
the secret necropolis of the Enlightenment which is like a Saint-
Denis built of philosophers' stone where one will be gently laid
between Sade and Lautréamont, the great captains, the men of
anger who have no more anger—and in the Luxembourg, draw-
ing up a chair to sit near the statues of queens and the girls who
pass, they stop suddenly, they are searching for where all their
anger has gone, then they smile, set off again, they tell themselves they still love Rimbaud, that all is not lost. André Breton
under the trees says his devotions and takes a seat near the
queens. Or again, if it is December and too cold in the Luxembourg, they walk down boulevard Saint-Michel in the north
wind, cross the bridge, enter Notre Dame, which is an excellent
windbreak, and there, in the dark of December, under the dark
vaults, behind a pillar, they suddenly see the enormous roaring
column of fire; and of course at that fire for sixty years they light a
work beyond meaning, ridiculous, prodigious, through which
stride great fiery captains who speak directly to God and whom
God calls by their ridiculous, prodigious names, *Thomas Pollock
Nageoire, Monsieur de Coûfontaine et Dormant*—but when they
take it into their heads to write a preface to Rimbaud and their
great wings have fallen off, there they are, nightingales, they mis-
take the pedal of charity for that of anger and quote the saints of

the almanac. They become Banville again. Even Breton and Claudel become Banville again and reply to Rimbaud wearing a silk skullcap over their white mane at their poet's desk.

■

All these books written on Rimbaud, that one book, in truth, as they are so much alike, interchangeable, however ludicrously at odds, like the successive interpretations of the *Filioque* in the Middle Ages, all these books come from the hand of the Gilles. The Gilles is better informed than Banville; he has been informed by a century of work; he knows more about the life of Rimbaud than Rimbaud ever knew, as has been rightly pointed out; he is more modern than Banville, with more modern resolution; floured and modern; he, too, is standing in a kind of garden, since that is where Watteau placed him: yes, he is standing in the Luxembourg, like Banville, like Mallarmé, like Breton with his magnificent mane under the leaves, like young Claudel at the moment when he pushes open the gate to rush down Saint-Michel and shut himself up in the windbreak of Notre Dame. Standing at the edge of that garden, where behind his back under the statues of queens there is laughter and games that he does not hear, some lovely afternoon where he is not, Italian pines, girls, the Gilles watches passing in the void the work and life of another, which he calls Arthur Rimbaud. He invents it: it is the magic that he is not. He watches that magic sparkle; he sees signs there, the promise of the Resurrection of the body or the gold of Time, depending; he watches the comet; he watches nothingness and salvation, revolt and love, the lowly body and the letter, which go at one another, embrace, dance, come apart, come together again, pass and collapse considerably. In his dark room at midday he makes that inexhaustible bobbin spin; that dance; that fall; and it leaves him dumbstruck, he who is nailed there with his arms hanging, his Caliban feet. Laugh if you like: but truly audacious, the most stupid of the Gilleses perhaps, is the one who dares to throw the first stone.

The Gilleses have seen *the considerable passerby*; they believe they have seen him pass; invented his passing; there where he passed they see a great furrow that cuts the field of poetry in two, rejecting the old-fashioned on one side, full of beautiful works of course, but old-fashioned, and on the other, the proud ravaged acre of the modern where perhaps nothing grows, but modern; he passed; and when he passed there they were leaning over their poets' desks and silently they speak to us of him, the horrible plowman, the white blackbird. They watch the comet; they note its winding paths; it has twelve feet and sometimes no feet at all or a thousand feet, that much they have found; they are looking for the place, the formula, and the key; they believe that it is coded; they combine those numbers; they are nearly there; they are going *to see*: and suddenly, if a sharper laugh rises behind their backs, if silk murmurs beneath the Italian pines, if a woman's voice as if from very far off calls to them in the great silence, they look up from their notebooks and wonder if the comet really did pass, if their mathematics mean anything, if poetry exists *in person*, or if it is the Harlequin who has rolled them in flour. Alas, Rimbaud has a talent for throwing flour in the eyes of those who approach him: and as I say this, my arms hanging, I begin to cough; if I beat my breeches, flour comes out of them. But sometimes I imagine, and all the Gilleses surely imagine with me, in the brief moments when we forgive ourselves, when we can bear ourselves, when for example the evening wind passes in those Italian pines that Watteau has painted behind us, when our colds are abating, when looking down at ourselves we no longer see flour but a kind of smock of light, then yes, in those moments we imagine that before us stands a tall boy who also had big heavy hands, working hands, like those of a *laundress*, says Mallarmé, a boy who to dust off his own flour beat his flanks to death with rhymes, the renunciation of rhymes, refusals, slave labor; who, to appear free, not of this world, not from Charleville, not born of the poor woman née Cuif, shut us into the modern slave galley—I imagine that this very weary boy is before us, standing there in his great clumsy shoes, he looks at us and lets his big hands hang. He is before us, the same size or almost, on his two feet; he comes from afar; there he no longer knows that he has created what we call a work; he has no more anger; greatly astonished he regards in our hanging hands the endless, futile Rimbaudian gloss. A thousand times he reads his name, then the word *genius*, then the old word *archangel*, then the words: *absolutely modern*, then illegible numbers, then again his name. He lifts his eyes to ours; and we remain there face to face, unmoving, dumbstruck, old-fashioned, the Italian pines behind us suspended in a breath of air, he is about to speak, we are about to speak, we are going to pose our question, we are going to reply, we are there—the pines rustle in a sudden wind, Rimbaud once again has leapt into his dance, there we are all alone, pen in hand.

We are annotating the Vulgate.

5

AGAIN WE TAKE UP THE VULGATE

Again we take up the Vulgate.

It is said that in the fight in which he struggled every inch of the way with Carabosse, since the inner closet may not have been completely sealed, Arthur Rimbaud sometimes ran off to lose her in the Ardennes countryside; that his long strides carried him into villages as formidable and dreary as cannon fire, handkerchiefs stuffed into the mouth, Warcq, Voncq, Warnécourt, Pussemange, Le Theux; that he was hungry for those places, for those handkerchiefs, for those cannons, and that the verses he strewed along the way said so; that he was hungry with ambition and tricked his hunger with little rhythmical pebbles, ogre and Tom Thumb, as his legend would have it. It is said that a longer escape, a dream, at the end of summer took him to Belgium, toward Charleroi by small paths with blackberries no doubt, mills among the trees, factories rising at the end of an oat field, and we will never know exactly where he passed or where his young mind seized upon some quatrain now better known in this world than Charleroi, where he was left holding the laces of his big shoes under the Big Dipper, but we know that, returning, he stopped in Douai, at the home of Izambard's aunts, three

gentle Fates at the far end of a large garden, fussy old seam-
stresses, and that those days in the large garden at the end of
summer were the loveliest days of his life, perhaps the only
lovely ones. It is also said that in that garden he made the poem
every child knows, in which he calls his stars like one whistles for
one's dogs, in which he caresses the Big Dipper and lies down
beside it; and that summer's end was all rhythm, usually twelve
feet, and Rimbaud, suspended on the rod in the northern sky but
at the same time with his two feet under the table in the green
inn, got all that onto the rod at one time, the pretty girl serving
the ham, the arbor where he eats it, and the North Star rising
overhead. And it is pure happiness. It is the very simple appearance of truth, which resembles God or a little dead girl,
behind a bank of flowers in September. It is said that two escapes
especially, without stars this time, far from gardens, far from
truth, took him to Paris. And no one was waiting for him.

There is dispute over whether he took part in the insurrection of the Commune; if he had the pleasure and the terror of
holding at rifle point a sworn enemy, evil in person, that is also
to say, a poor devil from the depths of the country to whom
Monsieur Thiers in Versailles had entrusted plume and rifle,
and if, with the deafening beat of the two antithetical cymbals in
his heart, he shot; or if he was the little drummer boy perched
on the barricade; and if below the barricade he ate soup with the
poor, the obscene, the gentle idiots, if he smoked tobacco with
them; we would like to believe so, but it does not really seem as
though we can, that story is in *Les Misérables*, by the Old Man,

not in the life of Arthur Rimbaud. Member of the Commune or
not, he returned to Charleville with the red spittle of battle like
grapeshot in his heart. It is said that from Charleville in May, on
May 15, he wrote to Paul Demeny, poet from Douai, author of
Les Glaneuses, whom the silver nitrates had also fixed once and
for all and transmit to us for reasons that have nothing to do with
Les Glaneuses, and in the photo on page 54, beyond Izambard,
beyond Banville, we see the poet's goatee, the little pince-nez,
the blown-back hair, the proud profile gazing squarely away
toward the blue line of posthumous glories: we know that he
sent to that famous addressee—whose fame was cheaply won for
having once received ten or twenty pages—the so-called Seer
letter; this is an avatar of the old justification of the poet, idealist,
voluntarist, missionary, magician—the bravado, the *pro domo*
smokescreen; it wears the new clothes of democratic Orphism
because it is meant to please, to please the poets of Douai and
elsewhere; and it is much more than that, because it is written
by a young man who is trying hard to believe in it with his whole
heart. But, bravado or stroke of genius, we read and reread that
letter, bent over our poet's desk, we answer it as Demeny did the
first time: because "to find a language" and "make oneself a
seer" are written in black and white in that letter—and those
things that had been in the air for twenty years or two centuries,
those things that had already been said, with more or less fan-
fare, by the red waistcoat, the Old Man, and by the other red
waistcoat, the one who truly wore the red waistcoat in the swell
of *Hernani*, Gautier, had been said too by Baudelaire, whose

waistcoat was long and dark, by Nerval, by Mallarmé, those things are said here in a more convincing fashion, more youthful, more warlike: and so it is right that at our poet's desk we tacitly agree that they were said here for the first time. It seems new to us, eternally new; but I want to believe with my whole heart that, for Rimbaud, it became old-fashioned poetics the very moment he put his letter into the box, maybe at the moment he signed it—although he tried to believe in it with his whole heart. It is said that he sent the young Verlaine a letter of the same kind, voluntary, provocative, superb; it is lost. It is said that Verlaine sank his teeth into that bait; and that at the end of another summer, in September 1871, for a third time a train hurled Rimbaud into Paris: but that third time, Cros and Verlaine must have waited for the *dear great soul* at the gare de l'Est, and Rimbaud, in the pocket of his too-short pants that showed his blue cotton socks, which we know exactly, socks knitted for him by Carabosse with a feeling we do not know exactly, perhaps love, in that pocket he had the impeccable homework, *Le Bateau ivre*, honed perfectly from one end to the other to please the Parnassus, and in the Parnassus to take first place.

On the gare de l'Est platform in a derby hat Verlaine enters the story, we know; and his own story here without the least hesitation firmly enters the Mons prison, the cask of absinthe and the tragic clowning, the pallet and the Golden Legend; and beside that pallet, nuns from the almanac and whores, young Létinois who was a tall young girl; but all of them, and wretched as they were, we see leaning over Verlaine, who looks to be lower than they are, as though brought down: because he was brought down and remained there, just as Izambard had been.

He did not need Rimbaud certainly, he was great enough to bring about his fall all by himself, and he had the will to do so; but Rimbaud was the good excuse, the stone over which fate stumbles. And more than anything in the world, Verlaine loved to stumble.

For the moment he has the derby hat, he sleeps in a beautiful bed with a beautiful wife. He alone knows that he stumbles with every step, he is young, it doesn't show yet. It is said that with or without his hat, stumbling or not, he pleased Rimbaud, and it was reciprocal: without dissembling, without any other ulterior motives except the one of being first, which they confessed to each other, we know that they each loved the writings of the other, believed him to be a *seer* or pretended to believe so— since it was the fashion of the time to imagine that in *seeing*, ineffable, secret, postulated nebula, the most distinct poems are born, the most beautiful planetary-like systems where trees grow in twelve syllables, where the universe is embodied; embodied a second time; and regarding that second incarnation each one told himself that perhaps the other had the key. Both were happy to note that the key, if it existed, was held by an accomplice to his liking. But we know that a few days after the gare de l'Est, both of them young and seething, they pleased each other in a different way: and it happened that in a dark room behind shutters they were naked before one another, erect, and short of cadences and numbers issued from clairvoyance, short of any poem, they joined; behind those shutters they stamped out the blind old bourrée of naked bodies, both of them searching for *the purple eyelet* in the other, and having found it, lashed themselves to it, and suspended on that mast that was not the rod, it happened that they shuddered and disappeared for a moment from this world, from the dark room, from the shutters of September, the body universally poured forth and nevertheless entirely concentrated in the mast, the eyes dead, the tongue lost. And that first bourrée that they danced together, of which we know neither the place nor the form, of which we all know the feeling, that movement of the great bedroom mast made as much wind in literature as the swell of *Hernani*, because men of letters are futile. However, there is no doubt about it, tempest or breeze, it passed over the writings of Arthur Rimbaud and improved them: because the young man had had a great hunger for that bourrée, for that eyelet that he may have been seeking the summer before in Charleroi and, not finding it, to summon it and to trick his hunger, he strewed little stones along the path: little stones are charming no doubt but do not suffice for the Work, which is of the race of ogres, and if the length of the rod, along with the pretty girl and the green inn, along with the Wanderlust under the rustling stars, does not also hold the dark ridiculous *purple eyelet*, then the rod is a bad alloy that will bend, as in the hands of Banville.

It is said that love won over their souls and went wrong, as generally happens when it wins over the soul; it is also said that, playing all the hands and all the roles, that of lover, accomplice, poet, they maddened the wife, the true one, Verlaine's wife, with the thousand tricks dictated by absinthe; for they were tricksters; they pressed down hard upon the E string of poetic destiny, the one, in short, upon which Baudelaire had pressed so hard that it had gotten stuck on the famous *crénom*; of the two, Rimbaud is thought to have pressed upon it more heavily; and as for the wife, she had going for her the old E string of Eve, who hears things differently; so that the Orphic puking on all fours at four in the morning on the conjugal steps incurred the old conjugal sanction, and the little wife pointed to the door. The story goes that the two poets, driven from conjugal paradise, after detours and drunken procrastinations with Cros, with Banville, at the Hôtel des Étrangers where the Zutists hung out, took the road east and transported elsewhere the luminous, stamping bourrée, still lively, although the worm of sentiment was within it; and that in Brussels and then in London, perhaps to rediscover the pure radiance from before the sentiment, they summoned more ferociously *the green fairy*, absinthe, the deep gold of whiskies, ales, the mud of stouts; that from the depths of those pubs, E string against E string, they were then seen in confrontation, flushed, the note stuck; and of course at other times well-behaved and studious the two of them bent over a single poet's desk in London, in dark, devouring London, like the very mouth of Baal, or the latrines of Baal, over which Capital was squatting behind its smokescreen, caught in the act—because that was the longed-for time of tough capitalism, when one knew who had to hold the gun and who had to be at the other end of it, which rifle butt to gnaw on, in which blood precisely to march; in that Old Testament London, sharing a poet's desk, one of them, I want to believe, wrote *Romances sans paroles*, the other *Chansons néantes*, which he later called something else, pieces wholly of grace, light as air, hardly existing, written in the mouth of Baal but very far above Baal and the mud of stouts; for then they pressed heavily on the E string, each for himself and for the dead; and at that desk in the lull they played jokes on one another, envied one another, forgave one another. Or they recited for one another those aery pieces, one standing, the other seated, like the girls for the king at Saint-Cyr; and the one who was seated heard grace and power and great rhetoric pass; and neither one knew that they would never have such an audience again, such a stage. But, the aery piece taken wing, they remained there (at least that is how they imagined the thing, the flight of the poem and the fall of the body, for in their souls they still surreptitiously wore the red waistcoat), they remained there, they donned their greatcoats and bravely entered the mouth of Baal, which is also its latrines, and in the depths of a pub they sank into stouts. The devout manage to recognize them in the midst of that Old Testament tar, they can easily distinguish what belongs to one and what to the other, here the seer, the innovator, there the poor devil attached to outdated notions, the son of the sun who walks in front, and the son of the moon stumbling behind; the devout have the gift of clairvoyance—I myself can see none of this: in the Babylon smog their features merge, which has the beard, which the scowl? It is too dark to decide which of the two is the mad virgin, which the infernal bridegroom: they have the same violence under equally black waistcoats. They are two identical devourers slipping easily into that pub; and the coachman who carts off what remains of them coming out of that pub at four in the morning takes them by the arms, picks them up, throws them as best he can into the back of the cab with their greatcoats all awry, the coachman above who speaks to the horses in the language of Babel and disappears, he wears the same overcoat. The whip cracks behind the smog, perhaps Rimbaud in the cab cries *merde*. They are going to the station, they are returning to Europe: because we know that they had a row finally over something to do with herrings; over that matter they left Babylon; and that, thrown back to Brussels for a second time, crazed, terrified, one of them, the derby hat, at three in the afternoon with twelve or twenty *green fairies* in permanent residence raging about since eight in the morning, went to the galéries Saint-Hubert and terrified bought a Browning, which was not a Browning but a 7-mm six-shooter, what make I do not know, and with it put a piece of lead in the terrified archangel's wing. And there he is entering the Mons prison and lying down, and the other one leaving for his Patmos, at Roche in the Ardennes, near Rilly-aux-Oies. In the inner closet, Verlaine is quietly stretched out beside Izambard. And the bourrée, insofar as it concerns them, is over.

■

It is said that they killed one another in that way because their characters were ideally opposite, like the sun and the moon; because one had the brilliance of the day, the ardor of the day, strength and the seven-league boots, while the other's aspiration was to barely glisten, to appear between branches, to set, to flee; because one fomented *la poésie moderne* while the other made do with old-fashionedness, that is to say, made use of that very old and effective mix of sentiment and end rhyme that, strangely enough, we customarily forgive Malherbe, Villon, and Baudelaire for using, but not Verlaine; also because Verlaine, indecisive and divided like the moon, did not give himself with his whole soul, was not entirely in London and had left a part of himself in Paris, from where the little wife sent letters and pressed as persuasively as Eve upon the E string. These characters are too strongly contrasting not to be false; we have retouched them at our poets' desks.

It is also said—to explain the herrings and the six-shooter—that they were consumed by the *derangement of all the senses*, to which they both earnestly applied themselves, because surreptitiously they both wore the red waistcoat; they applied themselves to it; they did not become seers and pursued clairvoyance in pure drunkenness, which so much resembles it: and we can well believe that ten months of shared bingeing turned two impetuous young men into the convulsionaries of Brussels, on the day when from the cauldron of stouts the muzzle of the six-shooter emerged like a flower. I do not believe in the nightingale argument according to which Rimbaud, aware of his genius, as we say under our silk skullcaps, scorned Verlaine, Verlaine's poetry, and accused him of being without genius; because Verlaine had genius; and Rimbaud, ravaged and incurable as he was, was modern with less absolutism than we are. But I do believe, as I have said, that in confronting one another, their respective E strings wore each other out; for both of them their little string, the Orphic E string, the string of poetic destiny without parallel, without measure, which Baudelaire had taught them both to play and which so easily gets stuck; upon which they pressed down hard; upon which you must play for yourself, convince yourself, and you cannot do so for long if another E string is squeaking next to you: for the simple reason that in a single room in Camden Town it is not possible for both to be *verse in person* at the same time. That cannot be shared between living beings, one of the two E strings must break.

And Rimbaud pressed harder.

Rimbaud played with greater care. He wanted to be poetry in person more strongly than Verlaine did, to the exclusion of anyone else: because that was the only condition by which he could hope to appease the old woman in the inner well, to allow her a bit of a rest, the dark fingers finally relaxed, the hand open, no more tampering, just the tenderness of sleeping flesh. In order to be consoled, to sleep, the old woman within needed the son to be the best, which is to say the only, and free of any master. Of that I am sure: Rimbaud refused and execrated all masters, and not so much because he wanted or thought himself to be one but because his own master, that is, Carabosse's, the

Captain, distant as the tsar, inconceivable as God, like them all the more sovereign for being locked away behind kremlins, behind clouds, his master had always been an ineffable phantom figure exhaled in the phantom bugles of distant garrisons, a perfect figure, beyond reach, infallible and mute, postulated, whose Realm was not of this world; and seeing the apparition of him in this world, not even the apparition but the suspicion, the appearance, the shadow, the lieutenant, the fallen incarnation that downed stouts into his beard and wrote beautiful verses, drove Rimbaud out of his mind, dispossessed him, and no doubt he was infuriated, at the height of indignation without knowing why, like a Pharisee whom the opaque God of the Law insults by appearing clearly as the filthy Nazarene. Verlaine wiped the stout from his beard and gazed, smiling, at this grown boy whom he loved; Rimbaud, indignant, spat on the ground, turned on his heel, and slammed the door. This refusal of a visible master, in Rimbaud's case, is called rebellion, juvenile rebellion, but it is very old, like the old serpent in the old apple tree, like the language we speak. It is in the language that says *I* when it passes over the heads of visible creatures and deigns only to address God. And the unfortunate Verlaine, superlative creature, who was only too visible with his beard and his jokes, who was twenty-seven years old, an established poet, recognized by the established poets, who knew the Old Man of the red waistcoat and kept in his possession letters from him, who had handled grand rhetoric for longer than a boy of eighteen, Verlaine, despite himself, could only appear the elder, royal despite his crooked crown, half-master: and he had to be brought down, for Rimbaud to be completely Rimbaud, the verse, necessarily imperfect because it served others, had to be broken, prose without measure had to be played with the greatest care on the little string, and one had to go off to die in the nothingness of the Horn of Africa, among tribes without violins, where one has no masters other than the desert, thirst, Fate, sovereigns all barely visible, buried in sand like the sphinxes, but sovereigns, captains, murmuring of ineffable commotion in the wind over the dunes, the phantom bugles of the wind. Thus on the way to that desert he brought down Verlaine; Verlaine who was nevertheless not Izambard, who had looked all that in the face, who knew that the Carabosse of combat dances in the heart of language and not only in old-fashioned Sedan or Capital; who, despite this knowledge or perhaps because of it, ran to the galéries Saint-Hubert, returned with a six-shooter to bring down language in person, to be its master, took two shots at language, who looked at him with the eyes of a child, sullen, clear, sovereign, all the while knowing even before pulling the trigger that one cannot bring language down, one cannot do it in, the bullet will ricochet and come back at you. And with that ricochet, he lay down, a rosary in his hands.

■

You are no longer listening to me, you are leafing through the Vulgate. How right you are. Everything is in there: the passions and the men, the aery poetry and leaden drunkenness, the high rebellion, the petty herrings, and even the rosary beads in Verlaine's hands, which Rimbaud calls precisely *un chapelet aux pinces*. And the luminous bourrée where it all began, the dance that they danced behind the shutters of September, that is there too—but regarding this chapter the Vulgate only makes delicate mention and holds its tongue.

It is the Vulgate, and it cannot be gainsaid, it is without flaw. It is beyond debate. Regarding this chapter however, the one on the bourrée, there is debate over whether Rimbaud's taste was only for men or for either sex equally, provided the emotion was there; if it was the Captain's shadow that he wanted to clasp once and for all or the unhappy flesh of Vitalie Cuif; we just do not know. And no doubt for the great magic sophism of twelve feet, which wants to die in London, nearly breaks, stops short, and in this waltz of hesitation beats like a heart, for poetry, the debate is pointless.

The Vulgate is without fault, and it is never more perfect than for this period, in London and Brussels, of pathetic love and the six-shooter; but it does not say how, from the point of view of verse, Rimbaud, who was seventeen years old, aged so much in those few months that it was as if in London he had written with a single stroke of the pen *Le Légende des siècles*, which was not finished, *Les Fleurs du mal*, which was, and the *Divine Comedy*—the one that could be written at the time of hard capitalism, in the ninth circle, the ultimate pigsty, in the clutches of Capital in person. Of that we know nothing. Of

Baal, the embraces, the poet's desk in Camden Town, of all that we are sure; and also of those more tender things that move us, their great youth, both of them, their puppy-like clumsiness, their puppy-like teeth, the hair that fell out by the fistful for one while the other wore his longer than they did in 1830, their hope and a taste for joking that they never lost, not even under the power-hammer of Baal or much later, after all the suicides. And those tendernesses allow us not to read the poetry, because no one can—except those who believe that it is code, and do they read further? We are romantic riffraff. No, we do not read, and I no more than the others. It is a poem that we are writing, each in our own manner, under our silk skullcaps, as one did in the past on the fine themes of Troy and Greece. It is our poem, and the poems of Rimbaud remain hidden within ours, kept secret, in reserve, as though postulated: our poem has so taken over that sometimes, opening the small book in which the writings of Arthur Rimbaud rest, we are astonished that they exist. We had forgotten them. Once again we glance through them, hasty, blind, fearful as the little ant that without regard for the lines crosses diagonally over our page, which we have put on the ground beside us in the garden.

In the garden we are glancing over those poems of 1872. We are imagining them. We think about their coming into this world for the first time, when a laundress's hand gave birth to those light songs, almost popular, popular young girl songs, where the old alexandrine hums that it must die and cannot resign itself to doing so, becomes two distinct verses of six feet, but remains. And it seems as if Rimbaud's heart is breaking in two as well: perhaps he knows now that there is no Salvation by poetry, no Awards Day with God the Father in the role of sub-prefect, and your proud young mother in her Sunday dress sitting behind the potted plants of paradise. We can hear it all breaking, his heart, the verse. It is the echo of a very distant battle that reaches us, the joint defeats of a provincial childhood and the alexandrine. The alexandrine has chosen to die with this little bugle. They are together on the knoll on the evening of battle. The old flag has gone into battle too often, now it is in tatters; both legs blown off, the old general hesitates. In this hesitation, his heart beats; the drums grow fainter; collapsed against a tree, he thinks of his battles, Saint-Cyr, Guernsey, and that now he must die; perhaps that is what causes this breeze of childhood, of early morning under summer trees, to pass over him. That is what murmurs within the little paternoster; and it is sung in tune because it is the childhood of Rimbaud that dies with the old general. He is wearing the little artillery kepi. Into his bugle he sings himself hoarse. That is what rings so true, what equalizes everything, the evening of battle and its dawn, the little ant and Eternity, the deep well and the stars, as in the memory of a man about to die. That is what marries the *seasons* and the *castles* without fuss, as time and space do every day that God makes, without fuss, June rises on a bright facade, and then it is already December. It is almost dark. We are watching the comet. Our hands hang. In the garden we stop reading, a little wind passes through the hazel trees above—suddenly we know, as if the breeze were saying so, that the death of the alexandrine is no more important or true than the popular Vulgate, that simple story of two young men full of *genius* who loved each other and shot each other. It is another Vulgate, the one about the alexandrine, hardly less foolish than the one about clairvoyance, that we have concocted under our silk skullcaps for the attention of our peers. An absolutely modern Vulgate.

Under the hazel trees once again we hesitate; we no longer know; we abandon the letter, we close the little book again, we return to the flesh of the poet that we will not know; we will not see the laundress's hand, without secret or clairvoyance or code, so simple, that sets down in a single line the *seasons* and the *castles*; nor the ardent patience and then suddenly the click, the exultant certainty of the hand that writes, leaves blank what must be blank, writes another short line, another one, stops, with certainty; we will never know if it is God or Baal who is making this hand move—and we pray that it is not Baal. If at that moment in the shade of the hazel trees we were permitted to see that hand as Verlaine saw it, and gradually above in the leaves the sulking face, the crooked tie, the tousled hair, if the mouth said *merde*, if more likely it was saying: *read*, extending toward us a poem with a begging, sullen, sovereign air, if before our eyes we read, we would know only what it is permitted to know on earth—what the ant knows who, without regard for the lines, is still running its way across my page, mute as the garden.

6

I RETURN TO THE GARE DE L'EST

I return to the gare de l'Est. I come back to those first days in Paris where perhaps for Rimbaud, it was all played out in three short acts: his immediate reputation as a very great poet, his keen awareness of the vanity of a reputation, and its devastation.

There was not only Verlaine. Because we know that in Paris in September from those first days Verlaine introduced him into the sort of cafés and caverns where, come evening, at marble tables, *glorias* steamed and pipes smoked, beers foamed, gazettes were opened, and behind beer glasses and gazettes in the paltry blue glow of gaslight, there were poets' beards, poets' poses, feigned impassibilities, feigned jokes, and poets' eyes that watched you arriving from Charleville. And behind all those screens in the depths of those caverns, at the café de Madrid, the Rat Mort, Chez Battur, the Delta, in the thousand annexes of the Académie d'absinthe, there was something else that Rimbaud immediately recognized, more quickly perhaps than he recognized which glass held the gloria, which the absinthe: there, almost stuck to their skin, was the ultimate screen generating all the others and in which all the others, beards, gazettes and beers, originated, a kind of screen of opaque sulkiness. In Paris the poet was that multiple man who sulked.

And each of those sulky sons was waiting for a father to come confirm his own sulkiness, to draw him from the lot, to raise him to his right hand on an invisible throne; each of them wanted to escape from civil society, not to be there, to reign by his very absence; but the monastery was closed, blue blood was no longer anything but folklore, the barracks had collapsed into the ice with the plumed sons, the marshals of the Empire, near Smolensk or on the Berezina; so all these sons, to indicate that they were orphans, exiles, that is to say, better than the others, all these sons became not captains, not barons, not monks, but poets; because that had been the custom since 1830; but since 1830 the song had worn thin; perhaps it had been sung by too many throats; too great a number were vying for the prizes from beyond; and most important, no one here below could guarantee them anymore: Baudelaire was dead, the Old Man conversing with Shakespeare alone in the four feet of his table, Saint-Cyr had long been without a king to have the last word, election was a thing of the past. The consecration that Rimbaud demanded with so much force, that all the sons no doubt demanded though less forcefully, that consecration was no longer in anyone's domain. And all those Rastignacs of the beyond were champing at the bit behind their obscure little sonnets and magic tricks, behind the beers and gazettes, waiting, sure of being the chosen one, sure of not being chosen: of course they all had the little cutting, but what was it worth when so equally distributed?

While waiting they had their photographs taken. Because

they were all aware that beyond the obscure sonnets, beyond
those little closed fists of fourteen lines brandished at the future,
beyond poetry, close behind the poses of exile struck with two
fingers in one's waistcoat, mane flowing, from under the black
hood posterity was hastening; and on the photographer's stool
they trembled before posterity: the Old Man before Nadar, before Carjat, looked at the black hood and held his breath; Baudelaire before Nadar, Carjat, held his breath; and before them,
too, gentle Mallarmé held his breath; and in the same way,
Dierx, Blémont, Creissels, and Coppée trembled before Nadar,
before Carjat. And Rimbaud himself . . .

■

It is evening, October. Not exactly evening, a very beautiful
afternoon in late October. It is Sunday in Montmartre, and as it
is almost in the country there is no one on the sloping streets. So
many trees there: chestnut or plane trees that dazzle and wring
the heart, yellow and ruined against the blue sky. They are
standing in the light. The golden leaves are racing beneath your
feet, the slope seems to lead you into the sky—and suddenly
there they are: there are four or five of them climbing the slope,
young, all hopeless sons, neither monks nor captains though all
draped in invisible frocks, simply sons, *poets* as they were called;
Verlaine and Rimbaud, and then whoever else, Forain, Valade
or Cros, and Richepin—whom they call Richoppe. Black
clothes, hats, neat appearances, all that resolved into flashes of

black under the sun; because that day they are well-dressed: someone has lent Rimbaud the uniform, someone his height, perhaps Richepin. The tie is a little crooked, but it is all there, the shirt, the polished shoes, and the opera hat, the tall cylinder on the head of poetry in person, the cylinder that has itself the air of being poetry, all the trappings of the distressed sons of the third generation—but not *the piece of vermilion Chinese satin* that would go so well with those leaves, not the red waistcoat, which was worn to the premiere of *Hernani* for only three hours and only once, just time for History to hold it in its opera glasses. It is no longer worn: moreover, at that same time the fine red waistcoat, swollen, sunk into his edema under the little red and white woolen bonnet, Gautier, between his swollen eyelids hardly sees you and does not recognize you, he is listening to a more powerful swell than that of *Hernani*; he is going to die this twenty-third of October, tomorrow or the next day, his swelling will not have gone down when he is carried into the Mont-martre cemetery, it is very close, and I want to believe that the sons, equally well-dressed, will be there, they will say that he was an old scoundrel, they will laugh aloud and be upset, between wines they will hear the swells of *Hernani*. Perhaps Rimbaud will think of Izambard, when Izambard offered him *Émaux et camées*. They are climbing rue Notre-Dame-de-Lorette in full light. They are smoking pipes which soothe their hangovers, the leaves soothe them as well, these sons; Rimbaud says that he is bored stiff, he is gloomy. They open the door of number 10, they take off their top hats, they joke around: there is still an inner court, a veranda at the back, shining in the October light. They all enter. There they are.

They are at Carjat's.

Carjat is a son as well, though a bit older than these five. An uncertain son, but a son. We know—the books know—that he was from a modest family; that his mother was a concierge in the back of a Paris courtyard, with silk dyers, so a very deep and narrow courtyard, perhaps foul-smelling, with rich dyes in the gutter and a bit of sky appearing very high up, as though above the edge of a well; but we do not know if he had made a well within himself on the scale of that courtyard to hold his mother, the slim catalogue prefaces devoted to him did not inquire that far: since he is a minor son. He has no golden legend. We get a glimpse of him through those of the others, Baudelaire, Courbet, Daumier, and the Old Man, because of his veneration for them, which they did not return, because of his friendship for them, which some of them returned, because of the black box as well, into which he put them thanks to the silver halides. He has his letters of nobility: he is said to have been the only artist to follow the coffin of the forsaken Daumier—the only one with Nadar, Nadar his friend, his elder, his rival, his better. That is not the source of his fame, which comes from having assisted the light, the valves that reject it, that quickly let it enter, the chlorides that fix it, when on that October day, the oval portrait came into being, eighteen by twelve and a half, of which I am going to speak, as well-known as the veil of Saint Veronica; and sometimes his own name, Carjat, is even written under the oval

portrait, but below the other name, in parentheses, or in smaller
letters. He did not see that portrait become so well known, he
died in 1906; and in his lifetime he did not want to be known
precisely for that, but for being a son, an artist; who had the
presence and appearance of one; who wanted it known, that was
the rule; who missed his shot because, through hedonism or
despair, which can be qualities of sons, or through good sense
and reticence, which are not qualities of sons, he was not pre-
sumptuous enough to pretend his practice was the universe; he
did not realize in time that you must passionately embrace a
single mania, an *art* as it is called, but only one, keep at it,
fiercely shut yourself away with it, as though in a sack into the
bottom of which you have thrown the mother you have, the
children you will not have, all mankind, and on that great tram-
pling you must embroider the fine work that will change you
into the son everlasting. Because the work is of the race of ogres.
Carjat was afraid of devouring and of being devoured: so he had
pushed his mania aside a bit to make room for a wife and a little
girl whom he had by her; and since his mania itself, all alone
and monolithic, frightened him, he had cut it into pieces and
practiced many arts; he was a photographer, of course, but also a
painter and a man of the theater; and his dearest wish beyond all
these appearances was to be taken for a poet, since he believed
himself to be one and thus truly was one: mania, belief, desire,
which may have come to him in 1848, when he was twenty years
old, almost the age of Baudelaire, and had smelled the powder
like Baudelaire, like him had taken the insurrection for the

magic wand that gets rid of the fathers without enjoining you to become a father, like Baudelaire in those days, had soaked the red waistcoat once again, had carefully hidden it under the long black waistcoat, like Baudelaire, wrote orphan verses in the style of 1850. But unlike Baudelaire, whose friend he was, he had not seized the E string in time, in youth when it passes within reach *in the banners of ecstasy*, he had not seized and pressed upon it to the exclusion of all other tasks: so that, instead of pulling the black waistcoat tight and beneath it giving measure to the twelve feet, the mantras of the West, up to and including the *crénom*, that is, instead of being a poet, he was only an artist—a free man who had time, changed waistcoats, was not sure if the father was Nadar or Hugo, Courbet or Gambetta. He wrote verses and made photos. He was a second fiddle.

He sees the five Mallarméan miters in the courtyard under the sun and below them the flowing manes.

He was waiting for the sons, he welcomes them. He is also a tall strapping man, like Rimbaud (and for a moment it occurs to us that they had a certain style, three months later in the heart of winter, the day when they had a set-to in the old 1830 manner at the Vilains bonshommes, when Rimbaud wounded Carjat with the mythological swordstick). And indeed Rimbaud is pushed to the front and they shake hands, Carjat has been told by someone or other that today he must do a portrait of this very young man who makes beautiful poems and whom he does not know. And since he also knows that this budding genius is an awkward character, the host is immediately very affable, he wants to put him at ease for the photo, as is his habit. We do not know what they said in 1871. The opera hats are on the large hat peg by the entrance, leaning this way and that, another one perched on top. Perhaps they have a glass of wine. Carjat remains standing. Rimbaud must be seated, and he says nothing—but if we were there, we would clearly see that these preparations, the clothes, the Sunday delegation, the host's ease, annoy him: he is thinking of the armband and the kepi, when, by an impossibly slow train, a tired photographer turned up in Charleville, and your mother leaning over your arm checked the unlikely scrap of clerical lingerie, added pins and puffed out the lace. Rimbaud blushes. And underneath, below that ancient shame, that ancient love, he is afraid and sulks hard: because this time the photographer is not an insomniac vagabond just off a local train, he is a Parisian, a master. He has photographed Baudelaire.

Leaning over him, the master observes him.

There are the two sons, face to face: the one who has so far only written Hugoesque verse, but perfectly Hugoesque, and whose destiny is toppling, because he has seen all the men of the Parnassus and suspects that to be poetry in person is not to be first in the Parnassus or anywhere else, that it cannot be ratified; because above all he realizes that poetry descends, like rue Notre-Dame-de-Lorette, it is a slope come tumbling down that leads you to a hotel in Brussels—or to Guernsey before the séance tables, sovereign, magic, charlatan: the slope goes to Guernsey, if you are very lucky. Before that slope he hesitates. There is the one son, and the other, leaning over him, the photographer, who knows he is important and does not really know why, who thinks it is because he is an artist—whereas he is a pure agent of Time, irresponsible and fatal as *Monsieur de Paris*. He looks at his model. He sees that the tie is crooked: he sees what color it is, which we do not know. The waistcoat is red or black, that will not show, the photo is black and white. He tells himself that soon the tie must be straightened; and then no, this young man is a poet, it is right for the ties of poets to be crooked. On the hat peg by the entrance the hats gleam in the darkness. Rimbaud says something, something obscene no doubt because they laugh, everything blurs, in their black clothes they move in a little sun-light, they are standing. With a single movement they are all there in the studio.

October falls through the glass roof, the light is strong and blue. Surely the wind has picked up outside, the sky is even larger. There are tall plants in pots, the light brightens and burns them as well, more slowly than it does the silver chlorides, but with the same passion. The enormous camera is waiting on its tripod, in its wagon bellows. And that cannon on its stand, exactly crowned by its cylinder: great gleaming pieces of yellow copper and black Bakelite fitted together. Then the platform, the stool, the dark cloth behind. Rimbaud is sitting where Baudelaire sat. The second fiddles against the wall are facing him, they are giving their opinions—each one is hoping that his is the opinion of a first fiddle. Carjat comes back with the plates, he has taken off his jacket. He uncaps the cylinder. He is under the black hood. Rimbaud has written *Le Bateau ivre,* as if he were going to die, that is where his thoughts turn, even if *Le Bateau ivre* is not exactly poetry, even if he has filed it as smooth as possible for the Parnassus, nevertheless, he has done it. The axis of his neck stiffens. The sky above fills with brass. The golden leaves slide over the shining glass. Between him and the armband, between him and the well, cascade the hundred lines of the *Bateau ivre*. He launches into the opening, he descends the impassible rivers, then he runs, then he dances; his lips do not move; his mother rises. She is leaning over the scrap of cloth, she has written the definitive hundred lines of the Parnassus, she sobs and falls, she rises again and triumphs. She sinks and rises like a cork in water. From under the black hood Carjat says to move his head a little, this way, then that way. He does as he is told, in the head that barely moves fall the impeccable stanzas, the impassible stanzas fall line over line, like waves, like the wind. The hemistichs topple, the syllables flow twelve by twelve over the country girl, she cries and laughs aloud. She has written that. She has brought down the Parnassus. The sky above is as grand as a father. For a long time Rimbaud has held his breath. Carjat shoots. The light rushes over the halides and burns them. At this moment Rimbaud *longs for Europe*.

■

Everyone knows that precise moment in October. Maybe it is the truth, in a soul and in a body; we see only the body. Everyone knows the disheveled hair, the possibly blue-white eyes,

light as the day, that do not look at us but gaze over our left
shoulder where Rimbaud sees a potted plant that is climbing
toward October and burns up carbon, but for us, that gaze looks
toward the future vigor, the future abdication, the future Passion, the *Saison* and Harar, the saw over the leg in Marseille;
and for him no doubt as for us, that gaze is also on poetry, that
conventional specter conventionally verified in the disheveled
hair, the angelic oval face, the aura of sulkiness, but beyond all
conventionality there also behind our left shoulder and gone
when we turn around. We see only the body. And in the lines,
can we see the soul? In all that light, the wind passes. In the
passageway the miters lack luster and witness. The hands of the
second fiddles hang. They are quiet. They do not know for
certain that the set lips have spoken *Le Bateau ivre*, but they
suspect that they have spoken some lines: they have had their
photographs taken as well, on the stool they have recited to
death their second fiddle masterpieces. They do not know any
better than we do on which stanza Carjat took his shot, which
word he trapped; no, we do not know if at that moment Rimbaud *longed for Europe*. We cannot see the laundress's hands.
We cannot see the color of the eternally crooked tie.

Carjat makes other plates, which are unknown—he destroyed them later when the two of them came to blows. He
does not know that he has just made his masterpiece. The sons
are sitting on the ground and making jokes, Rimbaud has become withdrawn again, these poets horsing around like naughty
choirboys bore him stiff. Suddenly we can hardly see them.

They are not going to stay there all afternoon. That is it. Carjat goes by with his plates, there are the vats, the nitrates, no time to waste, the sons know the way. They take their top hats, the hat peg is bare and alone in the hallway. The sky lowers over the five sons; they are in the street, the October light is declining, the trees are moving, the golden leaves are flying in the simple rhythm of the wind. They are gems underfoot. Holding onto their hats, the flashes of black descend the slope full tilt. They cross Paris, seven times a star appears in the Big Dipper, they are in the Académie d'absinthe.

7

IT IS ALSO SAID THAT GERMAIN NOUVEAU, POET

It is also said that Germain Nouveau, poet; that Alfred Mérat, Raoul Ponchon, Stéphane Mallarmé, poets; that Émile Cabaner, musician; that Henri Fantin-Latour, painter; that Jacques Poot, Brabant printer; that beyond Suez, Pierre and Alfred Bardey, merchants; that César Tain, merchant; that Sotiro, lowly employee of the merchants; that Paul Soleillet and Jules Borelli, explorers; that Menelik, king; that Makonnen, *ras*, that is to say grand duke; that little Djami, gentle young minion; that His Grace Jarosseau, bishop *in partibus*; that six nameless black Abyssinians running toward the sea with a stretcher on their backs; that on this side of Suez the doctors Nicolas and Pluyette who officiated double quick with a saw in the Marseille hospital; that the priest Chaulier who, after the saw had done its work, offered the unleavened bread in that same hospital; that Isabelle, Rimbaud's sister, to whom in the depths of mortal agony he may have called for God, or perhaps for gold or minions, we will never know; that the two or three white gravediggers in Charleville, as nameless as the six Abyssinians; that many witnesses, finally, saw with their own eyes that mythology, when it was that tall young man who was becoming old and dying. That tall young man of the great blunted rages, who no longer had Virgil on his desk to foster his rages, nor Racine, Hugo, Baudelaire, nor little Banville; who, for that matter, no longer even had a desk; who instead had a workbench strewn with do-it-yourself guides, surrounded by those black and white men I have mentioned. And as such, all those with whom he was associated, like Izambard, like Banville and Verlaine, that is to say, who served as father or brother and who thus passed on the phantom bugle, all those men deserve a chapter here.

I will not write those chapters.

I will abandon those men.

You, young man of Douai or of Confolens, you have seen those men; you know them better than I do: getting off your motorbike in front of the library, removing your Walkman, entering the cool vaulted archways and proudly planting yourself in the arid hall where the referents sleep, you have asked the orderly on duty in the gray smock, the *assis*, for the little canonical iconography; looking down on him scornfully, rearranging your little lock of hair over your brow, and then perhaps feeling across your shoulders the motorcycle jacket ripping from the pressure of wings, you have asked not for the works of Banville, Nouveau, and Verlaine, but: the Pléiade edition of Rimbaud. Because you thought, reasonably enough, that you would find there, in the simple portraits of men who lived, the meaning that in the *Illuminations* whirls round and then disappears.

You have seen these men; you have interrogated their portraits in the little canonical iconography; and sheet after sheet those gazes that rested on poetry in person have leapt from the page toward you. Page after page under those impenetrable stares you have asked yourself what a witness is. You have meditated upon the vanity of the portraits assembled there, and nonetheless devotedly you have interrogated them. And those who do not appear on the page, the Abyssinian porters, the Abyssinian minion, the Brabant printer, you have seen in your mind's eye sharing some object with Arthur Rimbaud. Leaning over your shoulder in the Confolens library, I have looked at them through your eyes: if they were printers, I have seen them make the *Saison* into the small magic folio that is more satisfying than bread, and more disappointing; if they were poets, I have seen them in my mind copying out whichever *Illumination* had just been written, not being satisfied with it, and recopying that small whirlwind into which all language flees with the meaning that disappears, I have seen them gaping as Vitalie Cuif gaped in Charleville before the Virgilian spreads: in London we have seen Germain Nouveau look up in the middle of an *Illumination*, displaying the proud profile, the poet's beard, the melancholy gaze turned toward the meaning that disappears. If they were merchants, I have seen them with *Rinbo* the merchant laying out antelope hides full of meaning; if they were kings or grand dukes, I have seen them bargaining with him over cases of rifles, lead heavy with meaning. If they were painters, you have seen their hands produce the painting called *Le Coin de table*; you have seen them bringing off that fabulous group portrait in which all of them, the six poets who fell into the abyss, Bonnier, Blémont, Aicard, Valade, d'Hervilly, Pelletan, and the two poets

who shine among the stars, Verlaine and Rimbaud, are seated
on the same chairs, breathe the same air, have drunk the same
wine, have the same gaze variously cast there toward the blue
line of posthumous glory; right below the handsome Elzéar
Bonnier under his black miter, mitered by his hair only as in
1830, you have seen Rimbaud to whom in the end the miter
returned, the nimbus of History; and this enigmatic Last Supper
in which, unusual for such a painting, the Son among the sons
is not in the center of the sons, opening his hands toward the
sons, but toward one side and even turning his back a bit on the
others, this Last Supper of modern times has filled you with
wonder and a little anxiety. Thus if they were painters they felt
that and showed it, by chance perhaps, but, one would like to
think, miraculously. And if they practiced the obscure art of
nitrates moved by light under the black hood, I have seen them
a hundred times, and I want to see them one more time make
that portrait I mentioned, that mandorla better known now in
this world than the veil of Saint Veronica, more full of sense,
more empty, that most high icon in which the tie is eternally
crooked, the tie whose color remains eternally unknown. I have
seen Carjat, and perhaps we have all seen him, pensive, gazing
at that crooked tie, hesitating to straighten it before taking the
photo. We have seen Carjat at that vertiginous moment when
he tossed onto the scale the oval portrait that weighs as much as
his entire work, or just about. And Sotiro too, the little Greek
employee who practiced the art of the nitrates very incidentally
when his boss Rimbaud had told him before striking his pose

how the black hood was to be put on, through which hole to look, which bulb to squeeze, which blade to release, little Sotiro who resembled Tartarin and conversed with language in person in a very relative French, we have seen him in the banana fields fixing once and for all, standing and too far away, the incalculable figure of Rimbaud the boss; and beyond Sotiro bustling about the hooded camera brought at great cost from Lyon, lugged for so little across the deserts, we have seen the old Rimbaud gazing into the eyes of an old woman in Charleville for whom he intended the photo. These men saw him; these men conversed with Rimbaud; and whether between them it was a question of meters or rifles, I have seen them all go speechless, laugh unpleasantly, and then justify themselves, or pound the table harder—if they were kings or grand dukes, that is—when Rimbaud's fist hit the table. But I will not speak of them any longer.

For I think I have stated the only three ways a living being could react to the existence of this living being, who was or had otherwise been poetry in person—this living willful being, locked into his hatreds and all doors open wide to the infinite freedom of objectless loves, in whom the love and hate he had embraced had nevertheless found in the Word an object so perfect that the man, without ceasing to walk, to desire, and to curse, practically ceased to exist when the Word collapsed; I think I have said everything about the human courses of action that were permitted before him, if one wished to remain human: being incommensurably outdone with a single blow, pretending not to be and proclaiming aloud not to be, but looking away and giving up, as Izambard gave up; interminably answering him, commenting, that is to say negotiating, knowing all the while, however, that the deal is rigged, with each weighing the king who is in the poem throws his gold sword onto the scale, you have to start over, accumulate on your side years of wretched paperwork, and still the scale's beam does not move a hair: that was Banville's way, or rather the way of that multiple man whom I called Banville for the sake of convenience. And finally, to do him in, once and for all to oppose lead to the Word, as Verlaine attempted. And if there were other human postures, they have escaped me—although blind obedience has not escaped me, doglike admiration of a small being for a great being, which was good Sotiro's way; but that does not interest me here, because obedience is not a quality of *a man of letters*, I mean that it has no dealings with the eternal relaunching of literature.

Nevertheless, I would like to leave Arthur Rimbaud there in the company of Sotiro among the banana trees. There could be worse fraternities: good Sotiro trots along with the tripod camera on his shoulder, his short legs make it hard for him to keep up with his boss's mythological strides. Beside the palm gardens the boss disappears, there his perfect rhythms disappear, his repudiated rhythms, his *delenda est* and his taste for the word *merde*. And perhaps that is the word he cries once more from under the shadows where he has disappeared, but as if it were a joke, a caress, for the benefit of the good Sotiro. And there: behind Sotiro, in turn, the palms close, perhaps they rest under the banana trees, the boss sleeps, once more he tries in vain to sleep off the drunkenness of his adolescence, the servant watches him sleep. No one sees them. What calm. No bugle here, under this shade; but already in Paris the bugles are sounding, a new flag is hoisted with the name of Rimbaud on it, and no longer those of Hugo, Baudelaire, old-fashioned names—everything is ready for the work of the dark fairy: the loving prose of the appalling Verlaine, the abracadabras of the poets Darzens, Baju, Ghil, Montesquiou, Berrichon, Gourmont, part seers, part Limousin schoolboys, and soon Claudel shut away in Notre Dame, Breton fulminating his harebrained hierarchies, soon the benevolent tamperings of the poor appalling Isabelle. Already everyone in Paris recognizes himself in the little oval portrait as if it were a mirror: everything is ready for the hermeneutic tourniquet, the interpretation mill spinning around a work as small and closed as a fist, clenched like a fist over a meaning it guards, a work born of a life torn apart, cut off like a human fist. He is sleeping in banana fields. It seems that he is keeping quiet. Around that silence, the free-for-all has begun. And, since I have to add my two cents to that free-for-all, since I must have my opinion on the matter, I will add that I think that if he kept quiet, *if he amputated himself alive from poetry* as we have so obediently repeated since Mallarmé, it was because the word was not that universal pass that the young Rimbaud of Charleville had so ardently imagined—and he realized a little too late that gold alone had some chance of being that pass (I wish with all my heart, Arthur Rimbaud, that you really, physically, wore against your skin that magic belt of gold that some people attribute to you, and that in the desert it granted you all rights).

Finally, if I regretfully tear myself away from the romantic mirage of that golden belt, that attribute of Sardanapalus as though worn under a mamluk's red waistcoat, I would also say that perhaps he stopped writing because he could not become the son of his works, that is to say, he could not accept their paternity. He did not deign to be the son of the *Bateau ivre*, of the *Saison* and *Enfance* anymore than he had accepted being the offspring of Izambard, Banville, or Verlaine.

I am looking at the comet. Belt of gold, milky way, *beacons* who art in heaven, images.

One last time I take up the Vulgate.

It is said that after Brussels, with Verlaine in Mons, well before the banana fields, Rimbaud returned to the fold; that in an attic in the Ardennes, in Roche, right in the middle of the fields and woods where the peasants of his maternal line had laid down their lives in vain harvests up to Vitalie Cuif, at harvest time, this appalling young man, this brute, this small heart of a girl, wrote *Une saison en enfer*; that at least if he started it elsewhere, in the land of Baal, in the metropolises where civilization had fallen into the clutches of Baal, the smoky, futurist clutches, he finished it here, in this highly civilized rural hole, in the clear and ancient light of the harvests. And when they entered the kitchen between two cartloads of sheaves, the brother, the two little sisters, the mother with her face of December in the middle of July, when for example at four o'clock in the afternoon they granted

themselves a little shade, in the cool shade cut themselves bread
into cool wine so as to take up their busy dance under the sun
more bravely, those harvesters heard overhead the author of the
Saison sobbing; and in those sobs for a century we have wanted
to hear mourning, the loss of Verlaine, the collapse of literary
ambitions, the lead received once and for all in the wing; also the
mourning for *seeing*, for magic tricks to make the word appear,
all the futurist mumbo jumbo that the *Saison* disavows in plain
terms; but I wonder if those sobs, those cries, that fist beating the
table in time were not, beyond all mourning, a very ancient and
absolutely pure joy. If perhaps they were sobs of the grand style,
that once in your life grace happens to let you spill onto the page:
those that the right words tear from you when they pull you
forward, those that shatter you when the right rhythm pushes
you furiously from behind, and you, left dazzled in the middle,
pronounce the truth, meaning, and you do not know how but
you know that at that moment on the page is meaning, on the
page is truth; you are the little man who speaks the truth; and you
cannot get over the fact that in a *sad hole* in the Ardennes, at
Terrier des loups, close to an old woman, dark and insane, meaning has made use of your brutish hand, your brutish mourning,
your girl's heart, to once again appear in its old castoffs of words.
Its mantle of June. You burst into tears before that mantle. And
the harvesters below, soaking their four o'clock bread in their
wine cut with cold water, exchanging looks filled with conster-
nation over poor sobbing Arthur, were entirely wrong: because
what they were hearing was perhaps something like the echo

here below of the triple *sanctus* that for eternity the kings of the Apocalypse tirelessly repeat tirelessly gazing at the glory of God; and nothing tells me that the kings of the Apocalypse do not sob eternally, uttering truly the triple *sanctus*. It was that great racket the harvesters heard. But however true the *sanctus*, of course Rimbaud was not contemplating the glory of God; because he was born and was writing at the appalling end of the nineteenth century; thus before him on the desk there was only the vain glory of the right words, from which God had been absent for a long time. Thus what the harvesters heard at other times, when for example at dawn they soaked their bread in the same bowl as at four o'clock, but it was filled with coffee and not wine, was the other voice, very old as well, *ferrea vox*, the voice of iron, vehement, authoritarian, despotic, the voice of the old prophets cast upon the wicked earth, full of resentment that their least word not be the triple *sanctus*, charging God to show himself, insulting him, crying only to the azure void of dawn. And when he was not the little king of the Apocalypse, the little Jeremiah in his attic made a great racket as well.

We do not know exactly what the *Saison* is; we think we know only that it is high literature, because those two voices, the voice of the king of adoration and the voice of the furious prophet, which are all of literature, are fighting there. It is more commented upon than the Gospels; between the celestial song and the blasphemy we cannot see very clearly; it is a renouncement that does not renounce; the yes and the no are not disentangled;

and leaning over it in our silk skullcaps we are interminably disentangling that yes from that no. It is said that the entire West is halted by it; that all its contradictions churn there as in a mill wheel, shattering like water on the wheel, emerging again intact like water from the wheel. Like water in the wheel, we clearly see that exultation; we cannot decide if it puts an end to the West or once more relaunches it; but rightly or wrongly, we agree to consider it a miracle, at nineteen years old, in an attic in the Ardennes, to write this fistful of pages, hermetic as John, abrupt as Matthew, foreign as Mark, strict as Luke; and like Paul of Tarsus, aggressively modern, that is to say, risen up against the Book, rival of the Book. And of course something is missing: because that sheaf of pages has no evangelical model other than itself, its poor, empty self, which, though *an other,* was not really *the other,* the verminous, glorious one of Nazareth. Perhaps this *Saison* is an old-fashioned thing compared to the Gospel. What matters is that, now, it is one of our Gospels. The little Jeremiah won, he was stronger than literature even while remaining within it, he has caught us.

He wrote the *Saison.*

I can imagine him going out at night into the Roche courtyard when the harvesters are sleeping. He, too, has worked hard. It is July and the sky is full of stars; under the stars there are dark haystacks as in the story of Boaz. We do not see Rimbaud, who is there: his disheveled hair, wide eyes, big hands, all his features secret, guarded, as though postulated, in the cool shadows of the

night. He is crouching against that haystack. We can hear him.
He is saying sentences written in the daytime, with great emotion, incomparable to any other in the world since God left the
human heart. And if there are powers in the air, if, as the poem
of Boaz affirms, they particularly love to frolic during harvest
nights, they recognize that great emotion which they heard in
the past in Judea, Rome, and Saint-Cyr, everywhere where emotion has given rhythm to language. They know it. We know it as
well, we know that it exists; but we do not really know what it is.
We do not really know what is leaping in that willful man's or
girl's heart, in unison with the words that roll from his mouth.
The attentive, distracted stars twinkle. The voice in the dark says
the *Saison* for the stars. The big hands close, the emotion
builds, the voice gives way to tears. We know this emotion exists.
Perhaps it is a joy of December. Is it power? Is it to be master
over them all now, Hugo, Baudelaire, Verlaine, and little Banville? Is it war? Is it to have thrown down the device of twelve
feet that kept us standing, to have defeated the old protocol and
left us all without protocol, powerless and taciturn as haystacks
in the night? Is it the bitter joy of having made of the poem this
perfectly straight, dark, vain, taciturn thing, indifferent to men
as a haystack in the night? Is it glory, far from haystacks and
men, for the stars, as the stars? Is it June? Is it the *sanctus*? Is it
the sweet joy of having found the new prayer, the new love, the
new pact? But with whom? The stars are dancing through the
dark leaves. The house is darker than the night. Ah, perhaps it is
finally rejoining you now, embracing you, mother who does not

read me, who is sleeping with closed fists in the well of your room, mother, for whom I invent this wooden tongue close to your ineffable mourning, your sealed enclosure. For I raise my voice to speak to you from very far away, father who will never speak to me. What endlessly relaunches literature? What makes men write? Other men, their mothers, the stars, or the old enormous things, God, language? The powers know. The powers of the air are this breath of wind through the leaves. The night turns. The moon rises, there is no one against the haystack. Rimbaud, in the attic among some pages, has turned toward the wall and sleeps like lead.

PIERRE MICHON was born in Creuse, France, in 1945. His first work of fiction was published in 1984, and since that time his reputation as one of the foremost contemporary French writers has become well established. He has won many prizes, including the Prix France Culture for his first book, *Small Lives*; the Prix Louis Guilloux for the French edition of *The Origin of the World*; and the Prix de la Ville de Paris in 1996 for his body of work. He has also received the Grand Prix du Roman de l'Académie française for his novel *The Eleven*, the Grand Prix Société des gens de lettres de France (SGDL) for Lifetime Achievement in 2004, and the Prix Décembre (2002) and the Petrarca-Preis (2010).

JODY GLADDING is a poet and translator. The author of three collections of poetry, she has translated over twenty books from the French. She teaches in the MFA Program at Vermont College of Fine Arts. ELIZABETH DESHAYS is a teacher, translator, and specialized horticulturalist. She is the author of a study on bilingual education and the translator of Julien Gracq's *La Presqu'ile*. Gladding and Deshays won the 2009 Florence Gould French-American Foundation Translation Prize for Pierre Michon's *Small Lives*.